Kevin & Colin's Tales of Mischief & Mayhem

Millie

The Comment on the back Cover is yours. Thank you! Have fun
Robert

Robert Prior-Wandesforde

Published by New Generation Publishing in 2018

Copyright © Robert Prior-Wandesforde 2018

First Edition

The author asserts the moral right under the Copyright, Designs and Patents Act 1988 to be identified as the author of this work.

All Rights reserved. No part of this publication may be reproduced, stored in a retrieval system or transmitted, in any form or by any means without the prior consent of the author, nor be otherwise circulated in any form of binding or cover other than that which it is published and without a similar condition being imposed on the subsequent purchaser.

www.newgeneration-publishing.com

 New Generation Publishing

To Angela, Alex and Ben for making this book possible

Robert has two sons and works as a Beanstalk reading helper. The charity provides one-to-one literacy support to primary school children who have fallen behind with their reading. He has worked with many reluctant readers and has written this book partly with those children in mind.

Contents

Snakes and Parrots 1
Stuck 22
Whodunnit? 41
Game-on 58
Snowballs 72

Snakes and Parrots

A rare moment of peace in Kevin and Colin's house was shattered by the sound of a familiar tinkle.

"Mum, it's Aunty Alice," shrieked Kevin, having dashed to answer the phone ahead of his parents, "and she wants to speak to you **urgently**."

"That's odd," Mum mumbled to herself. "Hi, Sis, what's up?" she said, having grabbed the handset from her eldest son. "Are you at the airport yet?"

The ten-year-old could only hear one side of the conversation and struggled to make much sense of it.

"That's very bad luck. Will you still be able to go?"

Pause

"You want us to do **what**?"

Pause

"This isn't one of your pranks is it, Alice? I know what you're like."

Pause

"I don't know whether to believe you or not."

Pause

"Okay, okay."

Pause

"Yes, they probably will enjoy it, but..."

Pause

"Hang on, what did you just say?"

Pause

"How big is it?"

Pause

"In that case, **no**, definitely not."

Pause

"Oh I see."

Pause

"It looks like we have no choice then. See you shortly."

"What's going on, Mum?" asked Colin, who had also been listening in.

"You know my sister is taking her kids on holiday today? Well, unfortunately, their house sitter has let them down at the last minute."

"So what?" said Kevin.

"So she's got nobody to look after their pets at home," Mum continued.

"Does that mean they'll have to miss their holiday then?" asked Colin.

"No. It means she's bringing them **here** right now on her way to the airport."

"Whoa. Nice one. Haven't they got some really cool pets?" Kevin yelped.

"I guess it depends on what you mean by cool," replied Mum, sounding rather less thrilled. "We're getting five fish, one parrot and a massive snake."

"**Yesssssss**," cried Colin triumphantly. "Bagsy have the parrot in my room."

"You're welcome to it. I'm going to have the snake and fish," chirped Kevin, rubbing his hands together in glee.

"Hang on, that's not fair," Colin squealed.

Dad thought he better interrupt before a full-scale argument broke out. "Remember they're animals not toys, boys. You're going to have look after them extremely carefully."

"Don't worry, we will," promised Kevin.

"Hmmmm," murmured Dad, not entirely convinced by his son's promise.

******

Before their aunt had even had a chance to clamber out of her car, Kevin and Colin had rushed out of their front door and were peering through the windows to catch a first glimpse of the animals.

"I'm glad you're here. You can help me carry these bad boys inside," Alice said, smiling broadly.

"You bet," screeched Colin.

"You'll also need their food. Can you put this bag in the fridge please, Kevin. It's for Barry."

"Who's Barry?"

"Barry the Boa. Our friendly snake," Alice's son Edward piped up.

"You've got a Boa Constrictor?" asked Kevin in amazement.

"We sure have," Edward answered proudly. "And it's massive."

"That's amazing."

"Oh and before I forget, here are two **extremely** precious things. One for you, Kevin, and the other for you, Colin." Alice was speaking seriously now, carefully handing each boy a light brown egg as she did so. "You've got to look after these **really** well. Keep them warm **at all times** and you never know what might happen while we are away."

"Got it," Colin replied earnestly.

"Right on," added Kevin.

"Okay. We've got to run now," said Alice, thrusting a list of instructions into Mum's hand before waving goodbye. "Take care of Barry, Peggy and the fish and **don't** forget about those **precious** eggs."

"We won't," shouted Kevin and Colin.

"Have a great time," cried Mum, desperately trying to look cheerful as the car sped away. "And please come back soon."

"Okay, boys, let's get these guys settled in," Dad said when everyone and everything was inside. "You can have the snake in your room, Kevin, although you **mustn't** let it out of its tank under **any** circumstances. We don't want to find it roaming around the house in the middle of the night."

"Technically, I don't think snakes really roam," Kevin suggested.

"You know what I mean, Kevin. Colin, please put the parrot on the chest of drawers in your room and I will put the fish in the kitchen."

"But what about the eggs, Dad?" Colin enquired, cautiously clutching the oval shaped object he had been presented with.

"Let's put them carefully in the airing cupboard. That way they will keep warm."

******

Later that evening, just as Dad had settled down to watch another Premier League football match and Mum had fallen asleep on the sofa, there was a loud screech from upstairs. Colin was ordering everybody to come immediately to his bedroom.

"You've got to hear this," the eight-year-old squealed in excitement when the other three family members had arrived.

"I can't hear anything," Kevin complained after a few seconds' silence.

"What are we listening for?" said Mum, rubbing her eyes.

"Wait for it, wait for it," Colin instructed.

"Wait for what?" said Dad, beginning to sound a little annoyed. His question was soon answered.

"Good night, sleep well. Good night, sleep well."

"Did she just say what I thought she said?" Mum asked, staring in amazement at Peggy the parrot.

"Strictly, I would call it more of a squawk, but yes, I think so," said Kevin. Colin, meanwhile, was beaming with delight.

"What a lovely, polite parrot," declared Mum. "Perhaps this pet-sitting is not going to be quite so bad after all. Good night, Peggy. Good night, boys."

"Aren't you coming in to say goodnight to Barry?" Kevin enquired.

"Certainly not," said Mum, heading back downstairs.

******

The next morning didn't start quite as well as the previous evening had ended.

"**Ahhhhhh**, what's this?" Mum screamed, dropping a bag she had just removed from the fridge.

"Oh yes. I forgot to tell you about that," said Kevin casually, barely looking up from his chocolate-coated cereal. "It's a dead mouse."

"I can see that, Kevin. But what's it doing in **my** fridge?"

"It's Barry's breakfast, obviously."

"Don't be cheeky please, Kevin," Dad said.

"I'm not. It's literally what Boa Constrictors eat."

"Nice," chirped Colin.

"Urghhhh, Alice never told me that," said Mum, her voice quivering. "**I** can't touch it. You'll have to deal with it, Kevin."

"Okay, not yet though."

"Now please, Kevin," Dad insisted.

"But I'm just eating my…"

"**Now**," repeated Dad.

"Oh and by the way, there's another three in the freezer," Kevin stated, reluctantly clambering out of his wooden chair. "We need to start defrosting the next one soon so it's ready for him tomorrow morning."

"Great," said Mum sarcastically, throwing her arms up in despair.

Back in the kitchen with an empty bag a few minutes later, Kevin asked, "Mum, can I take Barry to school today for show and tell? I've told all my friends and they're desperate to see him."

"Be my guest, Kevin. As far as I'm concerned, the less time he spends here the better."

"Thanks, Mum. They're going to be **sooooo** jealous."

******

Kevin and Colin were immediately surrounded by a swarm of chattering children when they arrived at school carrying the heavy glass tank between them.

"What on earth is that?" Brian enquired in his normal inquisitive manner.

"Wow, it's enormously fat isn't it," tittered Stuart.

"Awesome," Mitch gasped, as enthusiastic as ever, standing on tip toes to look at the beast.

"It's bound to bite somebody and that somebody is not going to me," the permanently pessimistic Tony commented, moving rapidly in the opposite direction.

By the time the brothers had fought their way through to Kevin's classroom and plonked the tank on the table it was time for lessons to begin.

"Kevin, judging by the huge commotion you have caused, you must have something exciting to show us. Please go ahead," the teacher instructed.

"Thank you, Miss Blackwood," said Kevin, who enjoyed speaking in front of the class. "Let me begin by introducing Barry the Boa here and telling you what he eats..."

Ten minutes and plenty of gory details later, the teacher decided Kevin had talked for long enough.

"Okay, that was very, umm, interesting, Kevin. Thank you. Any quick questions anybody?"

Stuart's hand shot up. "Can I tell a snake joke please Miss?"

"If you must, Stuart."

"What's a Boa Constrictor's favourite lesson?"

"I don't know."

"Hisssssstory!" replied Stuart.

"Right, let's move on shall we," Miss Blackwood sighed.

Much to the teacher's annoyance, most of the pupils couldn't keep their eyes off Barry during the rest of the morning and were reluctant to leave him when the lunch bell rang.

******

Kevin and Stuart were the first to return to class having gobbled down their fish and chips.

"**What**! How could that possibly have happened?" Kevin cried, staring at an empty tank and a lid that had been pushed to one side.

"Perhaps Barry fancied some lunch as well," Stuart grinned.

"This isn't funny, Stuart. We've got to find him before anybody else realises he's missing."

"Find who?" Miss Blackwood said, wandering casually into the classroom while munching on a cheese and pickle sandwich.

"Errrrr, ummm, hmmmm," Kevin stammered, while Stuart shuffled guiltily in front of the tank, trying to block the teacher's view.

"Hang on, the snake hasn't escaped has it?"

Silence

"Kevin, please tell me the snake hasn't got out?"

"It wasn't my fault Miss."

"Stay exactly where you are. Don't move an inch. I'm going to tell the Head what's happened."

Five minutes later and the whole school was standing in the playground as Mrs Adler, the Head Teacher, explained the unusual situation. "I know it's chilly, but we are going to have to stay here until the snake has been found. A specialist snake catcher has been called and should be here in an hour or so. I should warn you that Boa Constrictors are extremely dangerous and can even be **deadly**. They wrap themselves around their victims to kill them. However, everybody should stay perfectly calm. There is absolutely no need to worry."

Several of the younger children started to whimper, while others looked angrily at Kevin, who remained reluctant to accept any responsibility whatsoever. "There's no point staring at me. It's not my fault the lid wasn't on properly.

It must have come loose when Dad drove over that pothole on the way to school."

"Yeah, right," Colin said.

"I knew it, I just knew it," Tony mumbled, shaking his head and desperately looking around for an escape route.

"I wonder how long it takes them to digest their prey?" Brian muttered unhelpfully.

"I've got to say, this is pretty exciting stuff," remarked Mitch.

It turned out to be two hours before the snake catcher arrived, by which time even Mitch was fed up of waiting around in a cold, damp playground wondering if a lethal snake was about to strike. Kevin, meanwhile, had spent the time pondering how incredibly unlucky he had been. The only good news was that it was almost the weekend when he hoped all would be forgotten.

After a quick search, the long-haired, heavily tattooed expert found Barry on the Head Teacher's chair, sitting there almost as though he was running the school. He then took great pleasure in carrying the huge snake into the playground, before proceeding to kiss it on the top of its scaly head. It was a party trick he had performed to the delight of many children in the past and was disappointed when it was met with cries of despair at Singkem Primary. "Miserable lot," he murmured to himself, before carefully returning Barry to his tank.

******

Kevin, relieved to get home alive, was not so pleased to hear Dad's news.

"We have a problem," Dad began as soon as the brothers walked through the door, accompanied by Mum and Barry. "The boiler has broken down and the engineer won't be able to fix it until Monday."

"No hot water for us then," Mum groaned.

"Also, the eggs will get cold in the airing cupboard. I'm afraid you're going to have hold them to keep them warm, boys," Dad said.

"What, all weekend?" moaned Colin.

"I guess so... as well as sleep with them overnight."

"Classic," said Kevin in despair, wondering if the day could get any worse.

******

Anxious not to crush their egg by lying on it in bed, both boys had had a terrible night's sleep when they emerged for breakfast the next morning.

"Are those eggs okay?" asked Mum.

"Yes, but I'm not," grumbled a bleary-eyed Kevin.

"Don't worry, Kevin. I've got something that will cheer you up," said Mum grinning. "You can clean out the fish tank before breakfast."

"Can't Colin do it?" Kevin pleaded.

"No, you said that you would look after the fish," his brother quickly pointed out.

"Okay then, what do I do first?" sighed Kevin.

"You need to disconnect the pump," said Mum, studying the instructions her sister had given her.

"This thing you mean?" said Kevin, putting his egg down on the side and yanking the plastic tube that delivered air into the tank."

"**Not that!**" yelled Dad, who had looked up from his newspaper a little too late.

"Whoops. I guess that's not meant to happen," Kevin mumbled, as he watched water gushing from the hole where the tube had been.

"Good one, Kevin," Colin remarked.

"Don't just sit there, Colin," Mum yelled. "Go and fill a bowl with water so we can put the fish in it."

"Where do I find a bowl?"

"I'll get it," Dad cried.

"Hurry up. The water level is dropping fast and I can't get the tube back in," shouted Kevin.

No sooner had Dad got up he found himself sitting down again, having slipped in the water that was now all over the kitchen floor.

"Right, I better do it," said Mum. "You start to fish out the fish," she added, looking at Colin.

"Good one Mum. Fish out the fish. I like it. Where's the net by the way?"

"**Aghhhhh**!" cried Mum

"Quickly," urged Kevin.

"I'm going as quickly as I can," cried Mum.

"Well it's not quick enough."

"That's no way to speak to your mother, Kevin," said Dad rubbing his back and leaning over the tank with the net. "Got one."

"Four to go," Mum declared.

"I've caught two this time," said Dad, plopping them both into the bowl.

"Hurry up, there's hardly any water left," hollered Kevin.

"I've caught the last ones... oh no... hang on... one's jumped out. Where's it gone?"

"It's hopping about on the floor!" Colin screamed.

"Technically, I don't think fish really hop," said Kevin.

"Thanks for that, Kevin," said Dad.

"Pick it up then," ordered Mum.

"**I'm** not picking it up," said Colin. "It's all slimy."

"Ow," cried Dad, rubbing his head having hit it on the handle of a kitchen drawer while bending down to retrieve the fish.

"Come on, come on," urged Mum, showing no sympathy.

"Come here, fishy... gotcha... in you go," said Dad, turning the net inside out and watching the last fish join the others in the bowl. "Phew, that was a close one."

"Now, before you say anything," Kevin said, anticipating some displeasure from his parents, "it wasn't really my fault."

"Well it will be **your** pocket money **you** will be using to buy a new tank today," said Dad.

"But…"

"Right, let's get on with breakfast," Mum said, keen to change the subject.

******

"Mum, where's my egg?" Kevin muttered as he watched his food being delivered to him at the table ten minutes later.

"What do you mean?" said Dad, staring at the egg cup, complete with boiled egg sitting on a plate directly in front of his elder son.

"No, I don't mean **that** egg, I mean **my** egg."

After a short pause, Mum and Dad looked at each other in horror. Mum was first to speak. "Where exactly did you put it, Kevin?"

"On the side, there," he responded, pointing to the worktop.

"You mean right next to the other eggs?" Dad said.

"Yes, I guess so. I was in a hurry."

Kevin then looked down at his egg cup and the penny dropped. "**Ahhhhhhhhh.**"

"Ouch," said Colin.

"Hang on, Kevin, we don't know for sure it was **your** egg we boiled," said Mum.

"What do you mean **we** boiled?" Kevin responded.

"Can't you tell by looking? Does it have any special marks?" asked Mum, ignoring her son's question.

"I don't think so. They all look the same to me."

"Okay, I think we'll throw that one in the bin and assume this one is yours," said Dad, hastily whipping Kevin's plate away and handing him an uncooked egg from the side.

******

Apart from a minor snake bite, the rest of the weekend passed off relatively peacefully. Much to the relief of Mum and Dad, the boys spent an usual amount of time in their bedrooms with the animals, while continuously holding their own egg. Nevertheless, Mum was still very glad when her sister rang the doorbell on Sunday evening. "I trust they behaved themselves," Alice said, looking at the snake, parrot and fish, all safely contained in their tanks and cage, having been carried to the front door by Dad.

"I must say, we've really enjoyed having Peggy," replied Mum. "You've trained her incredibly well. She's so polite."

"Thank you. It took a lot of hard work I can tell you. It would be so awful if she said rude things, wouldn't it?"

"I couldn't agree more," said Mum.

"Thank you," squawked Peggy.

"You're very welcome," said Mum in reply. "We're going to miss you. Please do come again, we'd love to have you."

"Toot, toot," Peggy squawked.

"That's strange. I haven't heard her say that before," Alice remarked, looking puzzled.

Then, just as she was wondering how the parrot could have learnt that word, Peggy squawked loudly again. "**Core. That's a smelly one!**"

Mum immediately whirled round to glare at her younger son, who was now hiding behind the kitchen door. "**Colin, what have you done**?" she roared.

"Who, me?" Colin eventually stammered through tears of laughter.

Judging by her expression, Alice wasn't quite so amused as her nephew.

Unfortunately, once Peggy had started referring to toots there was no stopping her and eventually Alice had to put a blanket over the cage and bundle the parrot into the car. Having also loaded up Barry and the fish, the boys' aunt was ready to leave when Kevin rushed up to her window holding the two eggs. "Don't forget, these," he said breathlessly. "We've looked after them really well, I promise. We've kept them warm all the time, even when the boiler broke. I must admit I thought Mum had boiled one of them yesterday, but I think it's all good."

"That's very sweet of you, Kevin, but you can eat those for your breakfast tomorrow if you like."

"Uhhh?"

"I do love a good prank." It was Alice who was giggling now as she put the car into gear and sped off.

"**I don't believe it!**" cried Kevin.

******

Munching on some bacon on Monday morning, having turned down the offer of fried eggs, Kevin was wondering whether he would be summoned to the Head Teacher's office to explain himself when he got into school. "What do you reckon, Mum? Do you think she will have forgotten about Barry by now?"

"I don't know. I hope so," she replied.

"I suspect not," Dad suddenly chipped in. He was holding up the local newspaper that had just popped through the letterbox. On the front page, above a large, colour picture of a huge Boa Constrictor sitting on a chair, the headline screamed:

Barry the Boa Bites Back
Deadly Snake takes charge at Singkem Primary

"I guess that's not good news," groaned Kevin.

"You're not wrong there," chuckled Colin.

Stuck

"Now that's something you don't see every day," mumbled Kevin to himself. He was looking at a fire engine, trampoline, remote control, at least one person from each of the emergency services, lots of people clapping, and his mother drinking a glass of golden-coloured liquid. All of them were in his own front garden!

And the day had started so normally…

"Kevin, I've asked you to get up several times now and you're **still** just lying there staring at your phone." These were the familiar words of Kevin's frustrated mother, briefly thrusting her head around his bedroom door, before rushing downstairs clutching a couple of greasy plates in one hand and some dirty washing in the other.

The ten-year-old didn't normally give much thought to the washing, drying, ironing and returning of his clothes, except when his brother's underpants somehow found their way into his cupboard. Kevin just couldn't understand how the white ring around the top of his black underpants could possibly be confused with the light blue ring at the top of Colin's black ones.

His day-dreaming was interrupted by Dad appearing in the doorway. "I think it's probably time to rise and shine now, Kev. We've got to leave in twenty-one minutes," he said, standing in his pyjamas and sounding as though he had been reluctantly prodded into action.

It's all well and good for them, thought Kevin, *but they don't understand that it's literally impossible for me to get up at 7.30am.*

A couple of minutes later, and midway through an article on the pros and cons of the next generation iPhone that Kevin was reading on his previous generation iPhone, he was disturbed by a simultaneous, ear-piercing shriek of "**Kevin**" from his parents.

He quickly concluded that this roar must have been sparked by his eight-year-old brother moaning that he would be late for school. However, the fact was they had only missed registration twice in the last week and on neither occasion was it his fault. On Tuesday, Mum had moved his history folder from its normal place on the kitchen table to his desk without telling him, causing an unavoidable last-minute search. Then on Thursday, Dad had cleaned his shoes, leaving them near the sink rather than right in front of the back door where he always put them on.

Twenty minutes later and Kevin was up and dressed, hoping the fact that he had slept in his school uniform overnight to save time in the morning would go unnoticed: it didn't! "Kevin, how many times have I told you not to sleep in your school uniform," Mum groaned.

"Six times," Kevin replied almost immediately. A worried look from Mum made him think that he had overestimated the number, but, no, on further consideration, he was sure that six was indeed the correct figure.

******

At 8.09am, four minutes after the set departure time, Dad was reversing rapidly out of the drive onto the main road. Kevin, meanwhile, was eyeing some fresh-looking homemade bread which, not for the first time, he mysteriously found sitting next to him on the back seat of the car in a plastic bowl. *If only it was white bread,* Kevin considered, *I might have eaten that for my breakfast.*

Unfortunately, the trio soon ran into some heavy traffic, which didn't please Colin one little bit. "I can't believe you've done this to me **again**, Kevin. Dad, you've **got** to start fining him for making me late," he said referring to the pocket money system his father had recently introduced.

Money was withdrawn for bad behaviour and although extra money was available for good deeds, Colin considered the reward "far too small to be worth the effort". Under pressure from his parents he had once agreed to sweep leaves. But having worked non-stop for ten minutes, Dad had refused him a break, leaving Colin no choice but to go on strike.

Looking in his side mirror, Dad was surprised to see Kevin's head hanging out of the window.

"What **are** you up to, Kevin?" he cried.

"I'm taking a picture," came the muffled reply.

"Why are you doing that?"

"I'm going to send it to Stuart so he can show the teacher."

"You're not making any sense, Kevin."

"Yes, I am. It shows how unlucky I've been."

"How unlucky you've been with what?" said Dad, his voice now rising a decibel or two.

"With the traffic, obviously," sighed Kevin. "Oh, and by the way – I told you, you should have taken the other route."

******

Finally at school and sitting in a dull assembly, Colin couldn't wait for break time when he could tell Brian all about the hilarious events of the previous evening.

"Hey Brian, guess what?" Colin said, rushing up to his best friend in the playground an hour later.

"I don't know," said Brian, pondering the question more deeply than Colin had expected. "You've just won the lottery and are going to buy yourself a Ferrari F40?"

"What? No Brian, I'm not. Why ever did you say that?"

"Well, you did ask me to guess," a puzzled Brian said, staring at an equally puzzled Colin.

"Never mind that, Brian. I've got something great to tell you. You know the drone I got for my birthday last week? I've learnt how to fly it," said a wide-eyed Colin, not giving his friend a chance to answer this time.

"Nice one," Brian chirped. "How did you do that?"

"Well, I just practised. But that's not really the point," said Colin, eager to get to the point. "I got it to hover right outside Kevin's window so I could watch him on the camera. It was so funny and I don't think he even knew it was there."

"So what was he doing?" Brian asked.

"I think he was doing his homework. Why do you ask? Actually, don't answer that. It's brilliant isn't it?" said Colin, deciding he didn't have time to wait for Brian's response as he had caught sight of another friend out of the corner of his eye.

By the end of the mid-morning break, Colin had convinced a more enthusiastic Mitch to come home with him after school to watch the drone in action.

Meanwhile, at the other end of the playground, Kevin was grumbling. "Do you know what Stuart, Colin's gone and bought one of those drone things with his birthday money and keeps flying it right outside my window. I even heard him telling my parents that he was going to hide it in my bedroom and then turn the camera on! I can't believe they let him get it. I told them it would be a disaster."

"Don't worry, Kevin," Stuart said trying to stop himself chuckling. "Perhaps you could try and grab it when it's close to your window next time."

"Hmmm, that's actually not a bad idea," Kevin murmured, a thin smile spreading slowly across his round face.

******

By 3.22pm, Kevin and Colin were waiting at the edge of the school car park desperately checking their respective smartphones for the time and any news of Mum's arrival.

"School finished two minutes ago and she's **still** not here," Colin announced loudly to both Mitch and Kevin. "I'm calling her right now."

Having heard the phone ring a couple of times, he was irritated to see a text message pop up that read, "Sorry, I can't talk right now." Colin grimaced and decided to switch to plan B – ring Dad. But, just as he answered, the family's familiar, battered blue car loomed into sight.

******

Back at home and having devoured several of Mum's delicious double-chocolate cupcakes, Colin waved his friend out into the warm, late-afternoon sunshine.

"Okay, let's give it a go," said Colin, carefully picking up the drone and tiptoeing round to the back of the house where Kevin's bedroom was. "You look at the screen on the remote while I fly the drone up to his window," he instructed, pulling Mitch closer so he could watch the screen on the handheld device.

"What can you see?" whispered Colin, not daring to take his eyes off the prized possession buzzing quietly above them.

"Left a bit, right a bit, up a bit... that's it, keep it there. Ha ha. Brilliant stuff. I can see right into his room!" Mitch chuckled.

"Is he there?" asked Colin.

Upstairs, Kevin, who had heard the boys leave the house, hadn't had long to wait for his moment to arrive. Sitting out of sight, right underneath his open window, he could now hear the drone. *It can't be more than a couple of feet away*, he guessed, jumping up quickly and making a grab for where he thought the flying menace must be. Unfortunately, however, he was just short and as he lunged further forward, Kevin felt his feet slip from beneath him on the polished wooden floor. Closing his eyes and fearing the worst, Kevin felt the inevitable bump sooner than he expected.

Meanwhile, directly below the window, the two boys heard a loud grunt and looked up. To their surprise Kevin's head and chest were hanging out of the window as he appeared to be balancing on his stomach, half-in and half-out of his bedroom.

"What are you doing, Kevin?" his brother asked calmly.

"What do you think I'm doing?" came the less than calm reply. "Get Dad **now**!"

"Okay, keep your hair on, I'll give him a call," Colin said, pulling out his phone and speed-dialling his father.

Two minutes later and the whole of Kevin was safely back inside his room, explaining to Dad what had happened, while insisting that the drone be confiscated immediately.

"To be fair, Kevin, it was partly your own fault," Dad responded. "But, I'll tell you what, I'll fine Colin if he flies the drone outside your window again."

"Or hides it my bedroom," added Kevin, quickly.

"Agreed," said Dad, heading off to give Colin the bad news.

He found his younger son kicking a football aimlessly around the front garden with Mitch and, feeling sorry for the boys, suggested that he entertain them by kicking the ball as high as he could for them to catch. Dad always enjoyed showing off what he considered to be his great ball skills and was pleased the boys accepted the challenge, agreeing to take it in turns to attempt the catch.

He started cautiously, making sure he made good contact with the ball but only sending it about two metres into the air. Mitch, hardly needing to move, caught it easily. "A bit higher this time," Colin urged. Another clean kick saw it rise four metres, with Colin wheeling away to his right to take a good catch on the run.

"**Higher!**" both boys cried excitedly. Dad agreed, sending the ball six metres up, nearly as high as the top of the house, but with a bit of slice as it partly hit the side of his

foot. Mitch ran backwards to his left, before diving theatrically to his right and missing the ball completely.
"Good try, Mitch," Colin laughed. A similar kick saw Colin make a better attempt but with the same result.

Dad was enjoying himself, feeling confident that he could kick the ball above the height of the roof this time. "Wow!" Colin exclaimed as he watched it soar into the sky, while Mitch tried to work out in which direction to move. As the ball reached its highest point and started to fall, Mitch waited with his arms aloft, the sun in his eyes.

After a few seconds fixed in this position, he realised he must have missed it altogether and probably looked rather silly just standing there. Lowering his arms and looking over at Colin, who he expected to be enjoying another giggle at his expense, Mitch was surprised to see his friend still staring skywards.

"**Oh no**," Colin howled. "It's got stuck!" Sure enough, Mitch could now see the football perched towards the top of the tall beech tree at the edge of the garden.

"Sorry lads," exclaimed Dad slightly sheepishly. "I didn't get that one quite right."

"You can say that again," mumbled Colin to himself. "Don't worry, I've got an idea," he shouted, running inside and returning speedily with a rugby ball. "We can throw this up and knock the other ball down."

"Okay, let's give it a go," Mitch replied optimistically.

Following a couple of attempts, however, it was clear that the boys weren't able to throw it high enough. "Let me try," said Dad, stepping forward purposefully and positioning himself where he thought he would have the best chance of hitting the football. "Nearly!" he said as he missed it by a couple of metres on his first try. "Right, this time," Dad said, holding the rugby ball and taking careful aim before throwing. "Got it… oh no… wait… hang on…"

Colin interrupted, "I hate to tell you this, Dad, but the rugby ball has got stuck as well now."

"Look lads, I think you are just going to have to give up and wait for the wind to blow them down," Dad suggested.

"But that could take weeks," protested Colin. "I've got a much better idea."

Five minutes later and Colin was standing beneath the tree on a trampoline that Mitch and Dad had pulled over from the corner of the garden where it had stood unused for several months. "Three, two, one, go," Colin yelled, gripping the end of a long broom he had found in the shed and starting to bounce up and down on the trampoline.

"That's it," Mitch said, encouraging his friend as he got a bit higher with each of his first few bounces. Soon, Colin could see that the top of the broom was getting quite close to the balls but, at the same time, he realised that he was unable to get much higher. At the top of the next bounce he threw the broom and watched as it sailed through the air in exactly the intended direction.

"**Unbelievable!**" Colin cried. Hope had quickly turned to despair as the broom had also settled neatly in the branches, the handle tantalisingly touching the ball.

Dad had had enough. Shrugging his shoulders and turning his back he headed inside without uttering another word. Colin, by contrast, had not. "What we should do now Mitch, is use the drone to have a look at what's going on up there," he suggested, rushing off to get the equipment.

"Are you sure this is a good idea?" Mitch asked when Colin returned with the machine in one hand and remote control in the other.

"Don't worry, it will be fine. I'm really good at flying this now," Colin replied, executing the perfect take-off.

"Okay, let's have a look," Mitch said, squinting at the screen after Colin had skilfully navigated the drone into the correct position. "They are all very close together, caught between two small branches. I reckon once we hit one of them, all of them will come down," he concluded. Suddenly, the screen flickered and went dead.

"What's happening, Colin?" Mitch asked urgently. The response was loud, anguished and not exactly encouraging, "**Noooooooooo**, the battery has died." It didn't take Mitch long to realise that the drone wasn't coming down any time soon either. They must have used up too much of the machine's short battery life flying it outside Kevin's window.

"What next?" asked Mitch, beginning to lose hope.

"Well, I can't leave the drone up there. I will just have to go and get a ladder and climb up."

Colin could only find a small step ladder in the garage, but used it to clamber into the lower branches of the tree. Once there, he remembered that he was still wearing his white school shirt, which was no longer looking quite so clean. *Oh well, it's too late now*, he thought, reaching for the branch above his head and trying to find a secure foothold at the same time.

As he got a little bit higher, it dawned on Colin that the branches were becoming too thin to comfortably hold his weight. He would have to think of another way of getting closer to the objects. "Mitch, I'm going to lower myself down and pull up the ladder. I think I can stand it on the lower branches and climb up it," he explained.

"Are you sure that's a good idea?" Mitch said, repeating his earlier words. Colin didn't reply as he carefully manoeuvred himself within the tree.

Having successfully grabbed the ladder, Colin was able to lean it against the trunk, balancing the bottom precariously between two branches. He started to ascend. Three steps up and the ladder began to sway. "Careful!" yelled Mitch, looking up into the tree. One more step and the ladder slipped a bit. Colin was sweating now, beginning to wonder whether this was sensible. He noticed that he now had a small rip in his shirt and had also grazed his hand. Some blood was seeping from the wound.

Another two steps and he was nearly at the top of the ladder, within about a metre of the drone. Everything then happened in a blur: the ladder rocked, slipped away from the trunk, toppled and fell. Colin, his eyes closed in terror, grabbed for a branch, felt his hand touch one and heard the ladder hit the ground with a clatter. He was hanging on to a spindly bit of wood by the fingertips of his right hand, his legs dangling in the air.

"If you move your legs backwards you should be able to stand on a branch," Mitch yelled. While continuing to hold on to the higher branch, Colin did as he was told and was reassured to feel his feet touch the wood. "Okay, stay right there," Mitch ordered as he ran into the house to get help.

After what seemed like hours to Colin, Mitch reappeared with Mum and Dad in tow. "What are you doing up there?" shrieked Dad.

"Can you edge slowly towards the trunk?" Mum suggested.

"I don't think so," Colin stuttered. "I'm too scared to move."

"Give it a go," Dad urged, trying but failing to sound calm.

"He's going to fall," Mum said, beginning to sob.

"How long do you think you can last, Colin?" Mitch asked.

"I think it's more a question of how long the branch will support his weight," Dad whispered, looking anxiously at the thin piece of wood his son was standing on.

"I'm calling 999," Mum broke in, yanking out the phone from the pocket of her skirt.

"Which emergency service do you require?" came the response immediately the line had connected.

Mum frantically explained that she was looking at her eight-year-old child stuck in a tree a few metres above the ground, holding on to a thin branch with one hand and standing on another that was probably going to break any second.

"Okay, you better have all of them," the operator concluded. "We'll be there in about ten minutes," she added, tapping in the address Mum gave her.

Those minutes were spent in a frenzy of activity. Dad and Mitch carefully positioned the trampoline where they thought Colin might fall if the branch snapped; Mum prayed; Dad rushed inside to pour her a glass of brandy; Dad, Mum and Mitch attempted to reassure Colin that everything would be all right and Colin tried not to look down.

******

A young-looking police constable was the first to arrive. Pulling a notebook and pencil from her belt and looking suspiciously at Mum and Dad she said, "I understand you have a boy stuck in a tree. Can you tell me exactly what happened? It wasn't some sort of punishment was it?"

"It's quite a long story," replied Dad, trying to keep his cool. "Can I tell you after we've got him down?"

The conversation was cut short by the wail of a siren, followed by the arrival of two rather stout ambulance men in the front garden. "Which one of you is the patient?" the shorter one asked breathlessly, looking at the confused group of people in front of him.

"He's up there," said Mitch, pointing in the direction of Colin.

"I don't understand. I thought someone had fallen out of a tree?" the other ambulance man said.

"No," groaned Dad, "or at least not yet."

As the ambulance men stared at each other, trying to make sense of the situation, another siren shattered the silence.

Three men leapt out of the fire engine that had screeched to a halt in front of the house. They pushed past the growing gathering of onlookers and joined the others in the garden, pulling a long hose behind them.

"Where's the fire?" one of them asked urgently.

"There isn't a fire," Dad said, scratching his rapidly balding head in increasing bewilderment.

"We were told that you had a tree on fire, close to the house," the most senior-looking of the three firemen explained, still desperately searching for flames.

Dad paused and thought for a second, trying to remember his wife's earlier conversation on the phone. "No, I think my wife said 'dire emergency' not 'fire emergency'!"

Before anybody could say anything else, there was a loud sound of cracking wood, followed by a desperate yelp of "help" from Colin. This triggered the emergency personnel to spring into action.

"Go and get a ladder," one of the ambulance men demanded of the firemen.

"Get ready in case he falls," the policewoman instructed the ambulance men.

"Go and comfort the family," a fireman ordered the policewoman.

With everybody in their correct places, the lightest of the firemen began to scale the tall ladder he had propped up against the tree. "Hold out your hand and I will grab you," he said after he had reached the same height as Colin.

"I can't," replied Colin, his voice trembling. "I'm hanging onto the branch so as not to put too much weight on the one I'm standing on. Oh, and I'm also desperate for a pee by the way."

"Don't worry young man, we'll have you down in a **wee** while!" the fireman joked. "Right, we've got a problem guys," he shouted down to his colleagues. "We're going to have to get the fire engine into the garden and use the ladder on the back of it to get him down. And let's make it quick, our young gentleman here needs the loo urgently."

"Great. Thanks for that. Now everyone knows," groaned Colin.

"Okay everybody, out of the way," ordered the policewoman.

Squeezing onto the drive, the vehicle turned left, straight across Dad's carefully tended flower bed, and came to a standstill in the middle of the garden. A second fireman then pressed a button on the side of the truck to release and elevate the ladder fixed to the top of the engine, positioning it as close as possible to Colin.

This time the tallest fireman expertly climbed, stretched out, grabbed Colin, threw him over his shoulder and descended. "Job done!" he exclaimed proudly as he reached the grass and plonked Colin on his feet, receiving an enthusiastic round of applause from the assembled audience.

******

It was at that point that a confused looking Kevin exited the front door and surveyed the garden. "What's going on?" he enquired. Dad quickly filled him in on the events of the previous hour, while Mum hugged Colin and Mitch shook hands with the fire crew.

"Oh I see. I was wondering what had happened to my tea," Kevin responded before adding, "You do know everything's still stuck up there don't you."

His words were met by a stunned silence as everybody turned to look back at the tree.

The fireman who had rescued Colin was the first to react. "Don't worry everybody," he said reaching for the hose. "We can turn this on and use the water to dislodge the objects. It should easily be powerful enough to flush them out."

"Let's do it," his colleagues replied as a hum of excited chatter broke out amongst the crowd.

A minute later and a jet of water was pummelling the branches. "That's it, they're moving," cried an excited Mitch who was now dripping wet have been drenched by the spray. The rugby ball was the first to fall, followed by the broom and then the football; each greeted by a loud cheer as they hit the ground. Finally, the drone was propelled violently up and out of the tree.

A split second before it happened, everybody except Kevin, who had turned his back to go inside, could see what was about to unfold.

"**Watch ou—**" yelled Dad, a little too late.

"Ow," cried Kevin, rubbing his head in pain and turning to look at what had hit him. Seeing it was the drone, he tumbled dramatically to the ground, making sure he landed right on top of the machine, snapping various bits off it in the process.

His face pressed against the grass, Kevin let out a quiet sigh of relief and waited for the inevitable reaction from his brother. It didn't take long to arrive... "**KEVIN!**"

Whodunnit?

It was 8.45 on Monday morning and all the children and staff of Singkem Primary School were crammed into the hall to listen to the Head Teacher, Mrs Adler.

"As most of you know..." she began in her familiar posh voice, "...now is the time when I announce what the annual school play will be and ask you to audition for the various parts." Mrs Adler paused briefly for dramatic effect before continuing. "I'm absolutely delighted to tell you that this year we will be doing a... **Whodunnit!**"

"What on earth is that?" whispered Brian, leaning towards Colin who was sitting cross-legged next to him.

"I haven't got a clue," said Colin, shrugging his shoulders and looking at Tony for help.

"No idea, but it's bound to be a disaster," his permanently pessimistic friend responded.

Towards the back of the hall, Kevin was equally puzzled. "What did she say?" he mouthed in the direction of Stuart.

"Something about somebody doing something... I think."

"Oh, right," said Kevin scratching his head.

Sensing the confusion, the Head Teacher explained, "For those of you who don't know what a Whodunnit is, it's a murder mystery. Somebody is murdered, a detective is called in to investigate, he or she interviews the suspects and then skilfully works out who committed the crime."

The hall erupted in excited chatter.

"Wow! That sounds awesome," cried Mitch, who was sitting the other side of Colin.

"Too right," shrieked Colin. "I know what part I'm going to play."

"I wonder how the person's going to be murdered?" said Brian, who never tired of asking questions.

"Well, I'm not going to have anything to do with it," moaned Tony.

Behind the younger boys, Kevin was also talking. "There's obviously only one person who can be the detective."

"Who?" enquired Stuart cheekily, already knowing what his friend's answer would be.

******

Back at home that afternoon, the brothers were desperate to tell Mum and Dad about the play.

"Guess what? This year's school production is a Whodunnit," screeched Colin.

"That sounds fun," Mum said.

"I couldn't agree more," added Dad. "I always say it's hard to beat a good murder!"

"So are you boys going to audition?" Mum asked.

"You better believe it," said Kevin.

"I sure am," Colin chirped.

"What part do you each want to play?"

Kevin and Colin replied at the same time, using the same two words, "the detective".

"What? You want to be the detective as well?" shrieked Kevin at his brother. "No way. I'm doing that."

"No, you're not," grumbled Colin.

Mum was quick to step in. "Oh dear. That's bad luck. I guess you'll have to let the teacher decide and, in any case, I'm sure there are more than enough parts for both of you."

Ignoring his mother and pointing menacingly at his sibling, Kevin hissed, "I'll see you at the audition, bro."

"Not if I see you first," Colin responded, clenching his fists and narrowing his eyes to look as mean as an eight-year-old possibly could.

******

A week later and the Head Teacher was speaking to the school again, announcing the results of the auditions.

"I know some of you will be disappointed, but unfortunately not everybody can have a part."

"It's going to me. I know it," whispered Colin. "The audition went really well."

"My staff and I have put a great deal of thought into our choices," Mrs Adler continued.

"I can just feel it in my bones," Colin muttered.

"And it wasn't easy, given the quality of the acting that we saw."

"I'm certain I was the best."

"I want to thank all of you who came along to the auditions."

"I mean who could possibly have been better?" Colin continued his monologue.

"And for those of you who weren't successful, please don't give up. We will be having another play next year."

"I wish she would just get on with it."

"Let me tell you our decisions."

"At last."

"The murder victim, who is called Mr Magnussen, will be... Mitch!"

"**Yes!**" said Mitch punching the air in joy and speaking more loudly than he had intended.

"Thank you for that, Mitch. I'm glad you're so pleased to be murdered! Okay, moving on, the four suspects will be Sharon, Tracy, Stuart and Brian."

"What's a suspect?" Brian murmured.

"Don't worry about that now," Colin replied. "The big one's coming."

"And the Chief Detective, Inspector Gnomes, will be..."

"Come on, come on," urged Colin.

"**Kevin!**" the Head Teacher announced in a loud voice.

"Uhhh. Please tell me she didn't just say Kevin?"

"Yes, she did actually," Tony answered. "But don't worry Colin. You're probably better off out of it anyway."

Kevin, meanwhile, was fist-pumping Stuart, looking smug and thanking those around him.

"Quiet please children," the Head Teacher said authoritatively, bringing her index finger to her lips to indicate that silence was required. "There's one final part for me to tell you about. We have decided to have an assistant to the Chief Detective. The character's name is Doctor Watman and will be played by... Colin."

"Unlucky, mate," said Tony.

"Hmmm. That may not be too bad," Colin declared, stroking his chin and thinking hard.

Kevin was pleased as well. "Cool. Not only have I got the main part but I also get to boss my brother around. What could be better?"

"Ah, yes. Nice one," said Stuart, nodding.

******

Over the next few weeks, the actors spent a large part of most lunchtime breaks in rehearsal, learning their lines and perfecting their roles. Progress was steady and Miss Blackwood, who had been put in charge of organising the play, was feeling increasingly confident as the big day approached. She was particularly pleased by Colin's very positive attitude, telling her colleagues that he was proving to be "quite the model actor", much to their surprise. The dress rehearsal, the day before the show, was nearly perfect, the only problem coming when Stuart refused to hold Sharon's hand.

******

The next day, just before the play was due to begin, Kevin and Colin were talking backstage in a rare show of apparent brotherly understanding.

"Colin, I must say you've been very good about, you know, me having the main part and everything."

"That's okay. After all, you're older than me and this is your last year at the school. In any case, I've enjoyed it."

"What, even the bits when I have to tell you what to do?" Kevin said, looking surprised.

"Hey, we better be quiet now Kev, everybody's starting to sit down."

"Oh yeah. I can see Mum and Dad. Typical, they're sitting in the front row. Good luck, Colin. Break a leg and all that."

"Break a leg? That's not very nice."

"No, it just means good luck," Kevin explained.

"Oh, okay. You too," said Colin. "You're going to need it," he whispered while smiling a mischievous smile.

Things were not so calm in the boys' toilets, where Miss Blackwood was standing outside one of the cubicles, talking in a quiet voice.

"Mitch, are you okay?"

"Not really, Miss. I've just been sick."

"Oh no. How are you feeling now? Do you think you will be able to..." Miss Blackwood's questioning was cut short by the sound of Mitch burping and vomiting again.

Tony, who had been sent to find Mitch when he had gone missing, was also in the toilets.

"I think you are going to have cancel the play, Miss. I mean, there's no way there can be a Whodunnit if there's nobody who has had it done to them in the first place... if you see what I mean."

"You're absolutely right..." the teacher said.

"Thanks very much, Miss," interrupted Tony, puffing out his chest proudly.

"...which is why you're going to have to play Mitch's part."

"What? Errrr. Ummm. No, I can't. I mean, I don't know the words do I."

"Don't worry, Tony. There aren't any. All you have to do is be murdered."

"Oh. Okay. Fair enough. But what about the costume?"

"I haven't put it on yet," Mitch groaned from behind the closed toilet door. "It's still on my peg."

"Right, that's settled then. Go and get changed please Tony, while I find somebody to look after Mitch. I will then explain exactly what you have to do."

******

Ten minutes later, the stage curtains finally jerked open and the audience could see somebody sitting at a desk, writing. A single, small lamp provided the only light.

"Very atmospheric," whispered Dad. "I like it."

"Shush," said Mum. "You'll put them off."

From the right of the stage a shadowy individual then entered, creeping up behind the person at the desk, holding a knife. The attacker raised his arm and, ignoring an unhelpful shout of "he's behind you" from a young child in the audience, stabbed the man several times in the back. The victim then appeared to scrawl on a piece of paper in front of him before slumping on to the desk. There was a sharp intake of breath from those watching and the curtain closed.

When the curtains reopened, the stage was brightly lit and two detectives, each holding a magnifying glass, were examining the body and looking for clues.

"Come here and look at this, Dr Watman," Inspector Gnomes ordered, gesturing urgently for his assistant to move closer to the desk. "What do you notice?"

"There seems to be some paper underneath him."

"That's right. Well done. Now pull him back carefully and see what it says," demanded the Inspector.

Dr Watman did what he was told, grabbing the victim under his arms and pulling him back into a normal seated position.

"If I'm not very much mistaken, this is Mr Magnussen's Will. It says who will get his money when he's dead." Peering through his magnifying glass, Gnomes then continued. "Look here, he has crossed some bits out and written something in the margin. Oh and what's this?"

"Is it blood, Sir?" asked Dr Watman.

"Of course it's blood. But what else do you see?"

"Is it a letter of the alphabet?"

"Indeed so."

"What do you think it means?" asked Dr Watman.

"I think he was trying to tell us something."

"And what would that be, Sir?"

"It's elementary, my dear Watman... the name of the murderer of course."

Doctor Watman gazed in awe at the Inspector.

By this point, Tony was feeling quite pleased with himself. He had stepped into Mitch's part to save the play, died superbly and even avoided giggling when Colin had touched his ticklish armpits. But just as he was waiting for the last few lines to be delivered before getting off stage, disaster struck: the inside of his nose suddenly felt incredibly itchy.

Just my luck, Tony thought. *I can't exactly hold my nose when I'm supposed to be dead. But what can I do?* While he was still considering the question, the answer was delivered for him by way of an enormous, involuntary sneeze.

"Achooooooo!"

In the brief silence that followed, Tony wondered whether, somehow, he had got away with it. Perhaps it had just sounded very loud to him and nobody else had heard. The subsequent tittering from the audience suggested that he was wrong, while Kevin saying, "Bless you, my son," probably didn't help much either.

The following scene involved Inspector Gnomes asking clever questions of the four suspects, while Dr Watman took notes and asked less intelligent questions. First up was Brian, playing the part of Nigel Magnussen.

"Are you or are you not the son of the victim?" enquired Dr Watman.

"Am I?" replied Nigel, getting the two words the wrong way round.

"Yes you are," said Gnomes, "and what's more, I know your father was removing you from his Will when he died. You wouldn't have inherited a penny if Mr Magnussen had lived long enough to complete his new Will."

"Wouldn't I?" responded Nigel nervously. "But how can you be so sure?"

"Because I am, quite simply, a brilliant detective," Gnomes replied without batting an eyelid.

Next to be questioned were Sharon and Stuart, alias Milly Magnussen and Derek Smith.

"Mrs Magnussen, were you very upset by the news of your husband's death?" asked Dr Watman.

"Yes I was and still am of course," wept Milly, dabbing her eyes with a handkerchief.

"I don't believe you," cried Inspector Gnomes aggressively.

"Why ever not?" asked Derek. "You can see she's crying."

"I can also see that you are holding her hand," replied the Inspector.

"But how can you? You are the other side of the desk and can't see our hands."

"Ah, but I cleverly suspected that you were more than just friends, which is why I asked you to come here at the same time. It's also why I positioned a mirror behind you so I could see what you were doing."

"Ingenious, Inspector," Derek muttered.

"I know. Thank you," Gnomes responded.

Tracy, playing Ms Norbury, was the final person to be called.

"Rebecca Norbury, can you tell me how you knew the victim please?" said the doctor.

"Certainly. I worked for him; I respected him; he was my boss."

"I think it would be more accurate to say that you worked in the same firm as Mr Magnussen, don't you?" Gnomes had taken up the questioning now.

"That's what I said isn't it?"

"Not quite, Ms Norbury. The truth is that you wanted Mr Magnussen's job. You wanted to become the boss and control the firm, didn't you? You could then pay yourself a lot of money... more than enough to clear your huge debts."

"How did you know about those?"

"That is my job," stated the Inspector, "and, as you have just discovered, I am very good at it."

"Wow, this is great," declared Dad as the curtains closed again.

"It is, although I think Kevin is coming across as a bit of a bully? I'm feeling sorry for Colin."

"Don't worry. It's just part of the play. The Chief Inspector always has to behave like that. Anyway, I can't wait to see who's done it, can you?"

******

When the curtains reopened for the final time, Inspector Gnomes was pacing around a room containing the four suspects as well as Dr Watman who was leaning against a fireplace.

"Due to my extraordinary cleverness, I now know that all four of you had a good reason and an excellent opportunity to kill the victim. But the question is, which one of you was it?" Gnomes continued to speak while glaring menacingly at each of the suspects in turn.

"Was it you, Nigel? You would have lost a fortune if your father had lived much longer. Or was it you, Mrs Magnussen? Things would have been much easier for you and Mr Smith if your husband was no longer around. Perhaps you, Mr Smith? You could have helped Mrs Magnussen kill her husband… or maybe you acted alone? And you, Ms Norbury, also wanted Mr Magnussen dead. That way you could have his job and pay off the money you owed."

Gnomes then paused, apparently deep in thought, before smiling and continuing to talk. "Luckily, for Dr Watman here and indeed for justice in this country, the victim himself confirmed what I, of course, knew all along." The suspects all gasped at once.

"By writing the letter 'n' in his own blood as he died a cruel and painful death, Mr Magnussen identified his murderer. It was **you**," Gnomes concluded with a flourish, pointing directly at Nigel.

When the round of applause finally died down, Colin seized the moment he had waited so patiently for over the last six, long weeks.

"**Nonsense**! We both know that's absolute rubbish, Gnomes," he began, to the amazement of everyone in the hall. "You think you're so clever, but you just got lucky with that 'n' thing. If you're honest, you didn't have the faintest idea who had actually murdered old Magnussen. And come to think of it, the 'n' could mean anything. Maybe it was the start of an 'm' for Milly or perhaps the 'n' even stood for Gnomes. Did you kill the old boy, Inspector?"

Kevin was going to point out his brother's mistake, but there was no stopping him now.

"Also, I'm fed up of you bossing me around. You may be older than me, but I'm much smarter. In fact, I'm going to leave you and start my own Detective Agency. Yes, that's what I'm going to do, and if any of you guys want my help…" Colin said looking at the suspects, "…you know where I am. I'll even charge you less than him."

Miss Blackwood had heard quite enough by now, rapidly shutting the curtains to the sound of Colin yelling, "Police, arrest this man." To her amazement, however, the audience began to roar with laughter. Looking up, she could see everyone was now standing, clapping and shouting "more". The play was a huge success.

******

Back in the car and driving home, Dad was talking excitedly. "Boys, that was absolutely amazing. I loved it all, but that twist at the end was something else. So original. I've never seen anything like it before. And the way you left us hanging, not sure of the murderer's identity, was brilliant. Quite brilliant. A Whodunnit without knowing who did it. Incredible."

"But Dad..." Kevin whined.

"Not now, please, Kevin," Mum interrupted, anticipating what her elder son was about to say and thinking it would be wise to change the subject. "Talking of Whodunnits, I want to know who's done their homework and therefore deserves a massive pizza?"

"**Meeeeee**!" Colin shrieked, crossing his fingers behind his back.

"Me too. I would **kill** for a Margherita right now," added Kevin.

"Ha ha, good one," Dad laughed.

"I'll think I will give it a miss, thank you," mumbled the third person on the back seat.

"Oh yes, we had better get you home first hadn't we Mitch," said Mum.

"Too right. We don't want him being sick in the car," Kevin announced. "That would put me right off my food."

Game-on

The football season hadn't exactly proved a huge success for Colin who represented Singkem FC, playing as a goalkeeper for the under 10s. His team had just one point from nine matches, leaving it rooted to the bottom of the local youth league; the only point coming as a result of an abandoned game, which saw several players having to be pulled from ruler-length deep mud.

According to Colin, the absence of wins in the other matches reflected an extraordinary run of bad luck. A 5-0 defeat against Bridgeton, for example, was the consequence of "poor refereeing", while it was extremely unfortunate that Slea's skilful striker "was not injured" when Singkem played them last month.

But all was not quite lost. Singkem had one last match against local rivals Fordot to save the season and finish above their neighbours. Fordot had two points as a result of two weather-related abandonments, and were hardly setting the league alight either. Unlike Singkem, however, they had at least managed to score a goal against an opposing team, albeit accidentally.

******

On the morning of the big game, Colin awoke to the sound of wind and rain battering his bedroom window but was not going to let that disrupt his careful preparations. "Can I have scrambled eggs with my bacon, sausage and hash browns please, Mum?" he requested, entering the kitchen and seeing yogurt, fruit and various pastries waiting for him on the wooden table.

"How many eggs would you like?" Mum asked, reaching for the pan.

"Just the three today," Colin replied, wondering whether Mum had packed his bag for him yet.

"I've cleaned your boots and packed your kit," Mum said, seemingly reading Colin's mind.

"Thanks," came the unthinking response between slurps of orange juice as Colin began to visualise how the match would play out. He felt certain that today was the day he would keep his first clean-sheet of the season, while assisting Singkem's winning goal with a pin-point goal kick.

"Let's go then," said Dad, sounding as though he wasn't all that keen to head out into the howling gale.

"Kevin and I will be there shortly," Mum said, collecting together the half-time refreshments she had volunteered to provide and wondering whether her elder son had got out of bed yet.

******

The pitch was only a ten-minute walk from the house but that was more than enough time for Colin and Dad to get completely soaked, despite coats and the short-lived use of an umbrella that was blown inside out by the wind. Sensing that Dad's mood was not improving, Colin attempted to cheer him up by suggesting that he would enjoy watching Singkem's inevitable victory. However, his words were literally blown away by the wind.

Conversation was easier when the pair reached the relative haven of the changing rooms where Colin's best friend Brian was waiting for their arrival, bursting with questions as usual.

"How's it going, Colin?" he began.

"Good thanks, Brian. How are you?"

"Are you ready for the big match?"

"I sure am, Brian."

"Do you think we are going to win?"

"I sure do," Colin answered.

"How much do you think we are going to win by?"

"I reckon it's going to be 2-0 to us."

"Who's going to score?" Brian continued to probe.

"Trev and Mitch."

"How are they going to score?"

"Trev with his right foot and Mitch with his head," came Colin's speedy response.

"But what happens if Mitch gets injured?" Brian asked.

"Well, hopefully he will get injured after he's scored," Colin responded.

"What if he doesn't?" Brian persisted.

"Then you will score."

"Do you really think so?" Brian said looking pleased.

"Yes I do," said Colin, trying not to sound doubtful.

"Thanks, Colin. Nice one. But what happens if I'm also injured?"

Realising that this could continue for hours, Colin decided it was time to get changed into his goalkeeper's outfit. Clambering into his bright yellow shirt and black shorts he awaited the familiar remarks from his teammates.

Trevor was the first to respond to the sight of Colin in his kit. "Hey, it's highlighter-boy," he shouted, triggering the traditional giggle from the others.

"Well, I might look like a marker pen, but at least I'm not covered in sausages," Colin remarked, referring to the outfield players' shirts which were indeed covered with pictures of sausages. The team was sponsored by a local sausage manufacturer.

"But they're Porktastic," came the well-rehearsed reply, repeating the company's advertising slogan.

"Pass the ketchup," Mitch quipped.

The tittering was cut short by the arrival of the match referee. "Time for the toss guys. Who's your captain today?"

"I'll do it," volunteered Colin. "I'm feeling lucky."

Re-entering the changing room having lost the toss, Colin gave his team the bad news. "We're going to be kicking uphill and against the wind in the first half. But don't worry, it will be much easier in the second."

"We'll be exhausted by then," chirped the permanently pessimistic Tony from the back of the changing room. "We're definitely going to lose now," he added, holding his head in his hands.

"How much do you think we're going to lose by?" asked Brian.

"Not now, Brian," Colin said before Tony had a chance to give his no doubt gloomy prediction.

******

Outside, Kevin, who had now arrived in the car with Mum, was also moaning. "I don't know why I had to come to this."

"It's your brother's last match of the season and he needs our support," she explained, wondering where Dad was when she needed him to carry the heavy bag of drinks.

"But I'm going to get soaked and he's only going to lose... **again**," Kevin responded, dragging himself out of the warm car into the wind and rain.

Dad felt similarly gloomy standing on the touchline watching the Singkem players trickle out reluctantly from the changing rooms. The Fordot team were already on the pitch, looking cold but slightly more optimistic having received plenty of encouragement from a vocal set of fathers standing on the opposite touchline.

"Come on guys. You can do it," shouted Dad, trying to sound enthusiastic as Singkem argued about who would play as the main striker. He noticed several team members had gloves on, but was more surprised to see Tony wearing a colourful scarf and beanie as well.

Singkem's permanently angry coach had also spotted this, ordering Tony to remove the garments, before running on the pitch to all but drag them from him. It was fairly clear that the nine-year-old didn't like being treated in this way as he stood head bowed and completely stationary on the halfway line for the first few minutes of the match.

If that wasn't bad enough, Singkem were soon to suffer another blow. Walking towards his own goal, Trevor suddenly pulled up, clutching the back of his right leg before collapsing to the ground and rolling around in apparent agony.

"I think I've done my hamstring," Trevor reported knowledgeably to the coach as he hobbled off.

"Okay, I suppose you better go in and get changed," the tracksuited coach replied reluctantly, while looking around desperately for a replacement.

Dad could have sworn that Trevor was smirking as the boy passed him on his way back to the changing rooms. He also couldn't help noticing that his limp was becoming less obvious with virtually every step.

"Is Kevin here?" shouted the coach, running urgently towards Dad.

"Yes, why?"

"Can you ask him to get changed please. He can borrow Mitch's kit."

Before Dad had a chance to respond, the coach had turned on his heels and was jogging back to his previous position. *He's not going to like this*, thought Dad as he went to locate his son.

To his surprise, Kevin actually proved keen to play, sprinting out of the changing room in Trevor's tight-fitting, sausage-covered kit a couple of minutes after being informed. Colin, by contrast, was not so pleased when he saw what was happening.

"I bet you he'll be sent off within ten minutes," Colin announced to anybody who was listening.

"Why do you say that?" asked Brian.

"You'll see," said Colin.

"What will I see?"

As it turned out, Colin was wrong. It actually took eight minutes for the red card to be produced. Colin knew that what Kevin lacked in footballing skill he more than made up for in enthusiasm, chasing the ball like a headless chicken before diving in to reckless tackles. Having picked up a yellow card for a late challenge on the opposition's right winger, Kevin then accidentally head-butted Fordot's left-winger to receive his marching orders.

"Told you," said Colin to Brian as he watched his brother protesting his innocence to the referee, while several players tittered at the sight of a large rip that had appeared in the back of Kevin's shorts.

"Great stuff. How did you know that was going to happen?" Brian enquired, clearly impressed by his friend's prediction.

Five minutes later and Singkem suffered a third blow as the team conceded an own-goal, resulting from a back pass by Mitch. The ball had rolled through Colin's legs as he was slow getting down to the ball.

"It wasn't my fault," Colin insisted as his teammates looked at him accusingly. "It was Brian. He was distracting me."

"How was I distracting you?" Brian enquired.

"You were asking me a question."

"Was I?" said Brian.

"I knew we would lose," Tony piped up as he gathered the ball from the back of the net.

It seemed like a second goal before the interval was only a matter of time as Fordot mounted wave after wave of attack. Fortunately for Singkem, however, the opposing team kept shooting high or wide of the target, using up valuable time in the process as the ball had to be retrieved from the undergrowth. By the end of the first half, Fordot had had fourteen attempts at goal, zero on target and scored once. Singkem, by contrast, had drawn a blank in all three respects. In fact, they had only managed to get out of their own half once and that was at the re-start after the goal.

Returning drenched, caked in mud and thoroughly downhearted to their changing room, the Singkem players were cheered to see the feast Mum had laid out for them. "Wow, look at this guys," Mitch gasped as he eyed chocolate brownies, crisps, sausage rolls, biscuits and a range of fizzy drinks. Trevor was already on his second plate of food, while Kevin was sitting in the corner muttering to himself about the unfairness of his red card.

"Tuck in then," Mum said as the players circled the various delights, trying to decide where to start.

Singkem's coach didn't seem quite so impressed when he marched in to see what all the noise was about. "Go easy on the food, lads. This is not some sort of tea party you know. Remember we are here to win a football match," he barked.

"No chance," whispered Tony, just out of the coach's earshot.

"How are we going to do that?" questioned Brian.

"We go long. Just kick it and let the wind and slope do the rest. But make sure you kick it towards **their** goal not **ours**," he ordered, glaring at Mitch whose right cheek was bulging as a result of a whole sausage roll he had just popped into his mouth.

Ten minutes into the second half and the Singkem players were getting the hang of their new tactics. Hoofing the ball forwards at every opportunity and chasing it while shouting "charge", the home team were very much on top. Dad, peering through the near horizontal rain, also noticed that the Fordot fathers were not looking quite so confident now.

They were even more edgy when Singkem was awarded a penalty as one of Fordot's outfield players strangely decided to pick up the ball in his own area, tuck it under his shirt and run away. When the ball was finally retrieved and the coach had broken up a squabble over who was going to take the spot kick, everyone stood transfixed, waiting to see whether Singkem would equalise.

Mitch, chosen to make up for his earlier error, was feeling the pressure, not least from Tony who was telling him he was going to miss and Brian who was asking him which side of the goal he was going to aim for. Running up to the ball he changed his mind, kicked it to the left of the goalkeeper and looked up.

The good news for Mitch was the goalkeeper had dived the wrong way. The bad news was that he had underestimated how wet and muddy the ground was, meaning that the ball hadn't quite reached its target. It had instead stopped within a few centimetres of the goal line, very close to the goal post.

As Mitch pondered the situation, eighteen players rushed past him all heading towards the ball and all arriving at roughly the same time. What exactly happened next depends on who you ask, but three things at least were clear: the goal posts collapsed, the keeper's face was indistinguishable from the mud it had obviously fallen into and the ball somehow ended up over the line. Singkem had drawn level with two minutes to go.

"Hi. What are you doing here?" Brian said, surprised to see Colin out of his goal as the opposition prepared to re-start the match.

"I have a cunning plan," whispered Colin. "Go in hard at the kick off, get the ball, pass it to me and I will whack it as hard as I can."

"Then what?" Brian asked.

"Run like mad," Colin instructed.

Brian followed the first two instructions exactly but he too then under-hit the ball, giving the Fordot striker a good chance of getting to it before Colin. If he did, he would surely score and win the match for the away team.

Realising the huge importance of the moment, both players glared at each other for a split-second and then hurtled desperately towards the ball, straining every sinew to be first. The striker won the race. However, perhaps because he couldn't see clearly through the torrential rain, he missed the ball completely and fell flat on his face. Luckily, Colin didn't make the same mistake.

Still standing on the touchline, Dad watched in amazement as the ball, caught by the wind, soared into the air, flew over the halfway line, whistled above the heads of all the players, went through the goalkeeper's outstretched hands and nestled neatly in the back of Fordot's net. The stunned silence that followed was broken by the sound of three quick blasts from the referee's whistle, signalling the end of the match and the start of Singkem's celebrations.

Brian was the first to reach Colin. "How did you do that?" he asked.

"Oh, it was just something I've been practising," Colin replied, shrugging his shoulders and trying to sound modest.

"Pity you didn't do it earlier in the season," Tony mumbled as he joined them.

Mitch was the next to arrive. "That was incredible," he shouted, raising his hand for a high-five.

"Let's get him up on our shoulders," suggested Trevor, his injury now completely forgotten.

"Great idea," the rest of the team shouted, dragging their hero off his feet.

******

Dad had now been joined by a happy Mum and a not-so-happy Kevin. "You know we're never going to hear the end of this don't you?" Kevin began. "He just got lucky that's all and, in any case, that's the only match they've won all season. I don't understand why they're so pleased with themselves. Personally, I think **I** should be the man of the match," he continued. "After all, I was the only one who did any running."

"Yes, Kevin," his parents said, not listening to him.

Their attention had been grabbed by the sight of the Singkem players deliberately dropping Colin into a large patch of thick, sticky, brown mud.

"Oh no," said Mum, thinking about the state Colin and his kit would be in.

"Oh yes," said Kevin, his grimace turning into a broad grin as he imagined his brother's huge discomfort.

"Oh drat," said Dad, knowing Colin would be too dirty to go in the car and he would be walking him back home through the wind and rain.

Snowballs

It was snowing hard when Mum, Dad, Kevin, Colin, Stuart and Mitch arrived in the picturesque French mountain village for their first-ever skiing holiday. Mum and Dad had agreed that their two sons could each bring one friend with them on the trip. Kevin had picked Stuart, knowing he would make him laugh, while Colin had chosen the enthusiastic Mitch.

"Race you to the room," Colin shouted excitedly to the other three children once his parents had checked into the hotel and received their plastic keycards from the reception desk.

"You bet," said Mitch, accidently bumping into an elderly couple as he rushed towards the stairs.

"Sorry... er... excusez-moi," mumbled Dad in the direction of the pair, his schoolboy French beginning to come flooding back to him.

"Nous sommes anglais," Mum added, seemingly by way of explanation.

"What was that?" asked the heavily bearded man in a strong Scottish accent.

"Sorry, I didn't quite catch that?" Mum responded. "Can you say it again please?"

"We were asking you what you were saying, dear," the woman added in an even heavier accent, a mass of wrinkles appearing on her forehead as she frowned.

"Oui... er... yes," said Dad hoping this was the appropriate response, having not understood a word she had said.

While confusion reigned in reception, Stuart sped off in the direction of the lifts, with Kevin trailing reluctantly behind. "We'll easily beat them," cried Stuart, repeatedly pushing the up button.

"But I don't like lifts," Kevin whined as he watched the numbers in the indicator light above him falling slowly from two to one to ground.

"Don't worry, you'll be fine."

When the doors finally shuddered open, Stuart leapt in the cubicle, pulling Kevin behind him before he had a chance to escape.

"Which floor?" he enquired urgently of Kevin, his index finger hovering over the array of numbers.

As Kevin tried to find the answer from the keycard he was clutching, the lift doors closed automatically, only to spring open again almost immediately.

"Third floor, please," the Scottish couple politely requested as they carefully manoeuvred themselves into the cramped space.

"I hate to tell you this, Stu, but it looks like our room is on the ground floor," Kevin announced, suddenly sounding somewhat relieved.

"Oh no," shrieked Stuart in panic, frantically looking for the button that would open the doors again.

The boys finally discovered their two neighbouring bedrooms at almost exactly the same time, shoving the keys in the respective slots before throwing open the doors to loud cries of, "We won."

"No, I think you'll find I did," said Dad looking pleased with himself as Colin and Mitch burst into their room to find him standing there. He had just delivered their suitcases.

"Please keep the noise down, lads. Remember you're in a hotel," he added before quietly shutting the door behind him and heading into the corridor.

Colin quickly overcame his disappointment as he discovered the TV remote, dived on one of the beds, started flicking through the endless channels and turned up the volume having found a suitable cartoon to watch.

****

An hour later and the group of six had cautiously shuffled their way through the snow to the nearest pizza restaurant for dinner; the boys having all agreed that Mum and Dad's choice of a French meal was absurd. While they waited for their food to arrive, Stuart thought he would keep everyone entertained with his favourite snow-related jokes. "How does a snowman get to work?"

"By icicle!" Kevin replied almost immediately.

"How did you know that?" said a disappointed Stuart. "OK, try this one," he continued without waiting for an answer. "What do snowmen wear on their heads?"

"An ice cap!" came Kevin's speedy response.

"Uhh," grunted Stuart.

"I've got one," said Dad. "What's the difference between a snowman and a snowwoman?"

"**Snowballs!**" cried Kevin, loud enough for several people on nearby tables to turn and look in his direction.

"That's enough," Mum interrupted, glaring angrily at her husband.

"Hey. I've got a brilliant idea," exclaimed Colin, tucking into his huge meat feast pizza, topped with extra meat, that had just landed in front of him. "None of us have skied before, right. On our last day, let's have a race. Whoever gets down the mountain first wins."

"Oh yeah. That **is** brilliant. You're the man," cried an excited Mitch.

"Wins what?" asked Kevin.

"A delicious French meal for two perhaps?" Dad suggested sarcastically.

"I know. What about one of those **massive** Toblerones we saw at the airport?" Colin squealed.

"Nice one, Col. I like it. I like it very much," said Mitch, nodding his acceptance.

"Okay, you're on," said Kevin.

The elder boys didn't get a huge amount of sleep that night, meaning that Kevin's parents didn't either as their room was next door. The first interruption came when Kevin climbed into bed only to leap out immediately when he realised his bottom sheet was soaking wet. It turned out that Colin had somehow sneaked a snowball into the room and thought it would be "funny" to hide it under his brother's duvet.

A little later, Kevin and Stuart were in hysterics, taking it in turns to copy a French accent from a video they had found online. And then, just as everyone was finally dropping off to sleep, the silence was broken by the sound of Stuart farting loudly. The inevitable giggling that followed, broke into full-scale laughter and cries of disgust from Kevin as the powerful odour reached him.

******

The next morning at breakfast, a bleary-eyed Mum, clutching a cup of hot coffee as though her life depended on it, was not amused by constant references to the events of the previous night. To make things worse the younger boys had downloaded a "tap and fart" app on their phones and were busily trying out the various options, each accompanied by squeals of laughter and marks out of ten.

Dad, who himself appeared to be stifling a giggle on occasion, eventually had to threaten to confiscate the phones before some order was restored.

First stop after breakfast was the ski-hire shop. Being the half-term holiday, there was a huge wait even to enter the premises, while the group was greeted by a scene of utter chaos once inside. Boots, coats, skis and poles were flying in all directions, as everyone attempted to find the correct sizes and styles. The few staff there had largely given up trying to help, preferring instead to entertain each other with tales of past skiing and partying adventures. Dad, in particular, was not amused.

When the group of six was eventually able to make its way out of the store, Mum and Dad found themselves weighed down not only by their own equipment but most of the children's as well. At the same time, they were trying to get used to walking in ski boots, which was proving much trickier and more painful than expected. It all made for a sluggish, robotic march to the slopes, which was slowed further by an ice cream stop and a long search for a public loo.

******

"Let the skiing commence," Colin declared excitedly when the children finally entered ski school to be met by a smiling instructor.

"Are you guys ready to have fun?" the blonde-haired woman asked enthusiastically in excellent English.

Mitch was the first to answer. "We sure are."

"Well, let's get going then."

Before getting going, however, Stuart was keen to test out his snow jokes on a new audience. "What's a snowman's favourite game?" he asked the instructor.

The woman responded without a second thought. "Ice spy with my little eye!"

Puzzled but not deterred, Stuart was about to try Dad's joke when the instructor said, "I have a good one for you. What do you get when you cross a snowman with a vampire?"

"Frostbite!" Kevin said immediately with a smirk. Stuart just shook his head in disbelief.

Within half an hour, the kids had all learnt to ski in a straight line and were having huge fun seeing who could travel the furthest when starting at the top of a gentle slope. Kevin then had what he considered to be the great idea of attempting to take a selfie while skiing at the same time. "Look at me, lads," he exclaimed loudly, turning and raising his phone to take the shot, before falling, phone-first into the snow. Having shaken the worst of the white stuff from the phone, Kevin's companions were amused to see the resulting picture – a fuzzy close-up of his nostrils.

Dad, meanwhile, was not enjoying himself. He and Mum had been put into a group of twenty adults, led by a young, male ski instructor who was only interested in helping the female members of the party.

Also, although everyone had claimed to be a beginner, Dad was having far more difficulty than any of the others. In particular, stopping smoothly by making a "snow plough" with his skis was proving impossible for him. The two ways he had discovered to come successfully to a halt were either to crash into somebody or take a tumble. As bumping into complete strangers was proving rather unpopular with them, deliberately falling over became his only option, much to the amusement of the others.

Bruised and battered, Dad was desperate to put his feet up by the end of the two-hour session. But it was another two hours before he was allowed to do so. The slow trudge back to the hotel was interrupted first by a stop for creamy hot chocolates and then one for greasy burgers.

******

The next couple of days passed in a similar way, with the boys enjoying themselves immensely and Dad's struggles continuing. As a result, by the morning of the race, some of the party were feeling more confident than others.

"I'll eat my hat if I don't win," Colin declared at breakfast, munching on his second doughnut.

Kevin was quick to respond. "Ha ha. I'll enjoy watching you do that when I'm tucking into my Toblerone."

"Well, I don't suppose I'll win," said Mum modestly.

"You never know," said Dad. "On the odd occasion I haven't got my face stuck in a snowdrift you've actually looked quite good. One thing at least is certain and that is **I** won't be taking any chocolate home." Mum didn't disagree.

After ski-school and yet another pizza lunch, the group of six gathered at the chairlift which would take them up the mountain to their starting point. For once, the four children were quite quiet, concentrating on clambering onto the fast moving chairs as well as thinking about their tactics for the race ahead. The hair-raising journey took about five minutes and everybody was relieved to get off in one piece.

"What are you doing, Kevin?" asked Stuart as he watched his friend remove a box of silver foil from his rucksack and start wrapping the shiny material around his skis.

"I reckon this is going to make me go much faster," Kevin replied, continuing his work.

Colin wasn't convinced. "Good luck with that, bro," he laughed, winking at Mitch.

"You never know. He could be on to something there," said Mum. "I'm just concerned it's all going to come off and leave a terrible mess on the snow."

"Don't worry, Mum, it will be fine."

"Yeah, right. He always says that," whispered Colin.

With the six of them lined up and pointing in the right direction, Dad started the count down. He had only got to "two", however, when Colin pushed himself off to begin the descent. "Hey. That's cheating," cried Kevin. "Come back here." But it was too late, Colin was off and the others had no choice but to follow. All of them that is except for Dad. Realising that he had absolutely no chance of winning fairly, he had decided to let the others go, remove his skis and scarper back to the chairlift to catch a ride to the bottom.

Twenty metres down from the starting line, Colin had already opened up a sizeable lead on the others and was letting them know that by waving his hand while shouting "bye". He was followed by Kevin who was still complaining about Colin's head start, while Mitch and Stuart were neck-and-neck a couple of metres behind him. Mum was bringing up the rear.

Thirty metres down and Stuart, who was busily yelling "**Weeeeeeeeee**", hit a bump and lost one of his skis. Incredibly, he was able to continue on one leg for another few metres before hitting a second bump and losing his other ski. Even then, he managed to travel a further short distance before grinding to a halt, amazed still to be upright but cursing his bad luck to be out of the race.

Mitch then made the mistake of turning his head to see what had happened to Stuart. When he turned to look ahead again, his grin was immediately replaced with a look of panic as two people were skiing slowly straight in front of him. Trying to avoid them, Mitch fell on his bottom and twisted his legs, narrowly missing the couple with his skis but completely wiping them out with the rest of him. The three of them ended up in a heap on the hard snow.

"Whoops. Sorry about that," said Mitch.

"Ahhh. Why did you do that?" the elderly, bearded man cried in a strong Scottish accent, looking round at the culprit while trying to untangle himself from his wife.

"Hey, don't I know you?" the woman asked, rubbing her ankle in pain and staring quizzically at Mitch. "Weren't you the boy that bumped into us at the hotel?"

"Sorry. What did you say?" enquired Mitch, getting to his feet. "I really need to go. I hope you're okay," he mumbled as he set off in desperate pursuit of the leaders again.

About three-quarters of the way down and closing in on his brother, Kevin saw a large piece of silver foil flying off his right ski, quickly followed by another and then another. "I don't believe it," he said to himself as he started to veer off to the right. Having one ski with the foil still on and the other losing the wrapping rapidly meant his left ski was moving slightly faster than the right and he was out of control.

At the side of the run there were piles of snow which Kevin thought would stop him. He was wrong. Instead, they acted as a ramp, sending him flying into the air where he hung for a couple of seconds before landing neatly on a parallel run. As he slowly opened his eyes and breathed a huge sigh of relief, Kevin was speechless for the first time in a very long time.

Colin, meanwhile, was closing in on the agreed finishing line, near to the entrance of the chairlift, where the slope flattened out. He hadn't seen any of the others pass him and was feeling super-confident of victory. In fact, he could almost taste the Toblerone when he suddenly realised he was heading directly for the entrance sign to the ski school and had no idea how to turn.

Dad, who was on the chairlift looking down, could only look on with a mixture of horror and amazement as his younger son continued straight into the sign and out the other side, leaving a child-shaped hole in the cardboard.

Off-balance now and with his view partly blocked by a large bit of card that had somehow attached itself to his goggles, Colin swayed, wobbled, teetered and finally fell within a few feet of the finish. He was facing the wrong way and looked up just in time to see Mum steadily zigzagging her way down the last few metres and over the line. "**Nooooooooo**," howled Colin, spitting bits of dirty snow and ice out of his mouth.

When the party had reassembled close to where Colin had tumbled, Dad whispered, "I think we should get going... and quickly." Looking up the hill, he could see cardboard, silver foil and skis littering the slope.

"Yes, that's probably a good idea," agreed Mum, noticing the Scottish couple and several other angry-looking people heading rapidly in their direction. "But let's not make it too obvious shall we."

"**Run for your lives, guys!**" Colin immediately yelled, choosing to ignore his mother's advice.

******

It was only when the group was on the plane flying home later that day, that Dad started to relax again. "I don't know about you, but I'm ready to retire from skiing," he said looking at his wife for support.

"Certainly not," she replied with a smile. "The children enjoyed it, and besides, this Toblerone is absolutely delicious!"

The boys, meanwhile, were arguing about who was the best skier.

"It's obviously me. I was just unlucky in the race," explained Kevin. "I definitely would have won if the pizza restaurant had given me better quality silver foil to put on my skis."

"Hey, Colin. Talking about the race, shouldn't you be eating your hat now," said Stuart, reminding him of his earlier promise.

"I never said I would eat my hat if I didn't win," Colin claimed, his face reddening a little. "In any case, I lost my hat when that sign got in my way. I really don't know what it was doing there."

"That reminds me," said Stuart excitedly. "What do you call a snowman that tells tales?"

After a few seconds of head-scratching, Kevin replied, "Actually, I don't know that one. What **do** you call a snowman that tells tales?"

"**Yes**, I've got you," cried Stuart, doing several dabs in triumph.

"So what's the answer?" asked Mitch.

"Hmmm. Good question. I've forgotten."

"What. How could you?" said Colin.

"Only joking! A snow-fake of course!"

Stuart's punch-line was met by a groan loud enough to wake several sleeping passengers.

Lightning Source UK Ltd.
Milton Keynes UK
UKHW01n0831250818
327770UK00001B/26/P